School of Fish
Rocking the Tide

By Jane Yolen

Illustrated by Mike Moran

Ready-to-Read

Simon Spotlight
New York   London   Toronto   Sydney   New Delhi

SIMON SPOTLIGHT
An imprint of Simon & Schuster Children's Publishing Division
1230 Avenue of the Americas, New York, New York 10020
This Simon Spotlight edition June 2020
Text copyright © 2020 by Jane Yolen
Illustrations copyright © 2020 by Mike Moran

For information about special discounts for bulk purchases, please contact
Simon & Schuster Special Sales at 1-866-506-1949
or business@simonandschuster.com.
Manufactured in the United States of America 0520 LAK
10 9 8 7 6 5 4 3 2 1
Library of Congress Cataloging-in-Publication Data
Names: Yolen, Jane, author. | Moran, Mike, 1957– illustrator.
Title: Rocking the tide / by Jane Yolen ; illustrated by Mike Moran.
Description: Simon Spotlight edition. | New York : Simon Spotlight, 2020. |
Series: School of fish | Summary: A guitar-playing fish and his friends in a band
called the Fry are eager to perform in a school concert but they all have the jitters,
afraid something will go wrong.
Identifiers: LCCN 2019051233 | ISBN 9781534453081 (hardcover) |
ISBN 9781534453074 (trade paperback) | ISBN 9781534453098 (eBook)
Subjects: CYAC: Stories in rhyme. | Bands (Music)—Fiction. | Stage fright—
Fiction. | Schools—Fiction. | Fishes—Fiction. | Marine animals—Fiction.
Classification: LCC PZ8.3.Y76 Rk 2020 | DDC [E]—dc23
LC record available at https://lccn.loc.gov/2019051233

I'm silver. I'm cool.

I'm off to school.

My pencils are stacked.

My guitar is packed.

It's music day.

Our band will play.

We're called the Fry,
a fancy name
for little fish.
We hope for fame.

We will play
this afternoon
after practicing
our tune.

The shark bus comes.

My friends are there.

We joke and jostle,

but there's a scare.

We have the jitters.

Will fish kids clap?

Will clam kids let
their clam shells tap?

Or will they boo
when we're halfway
through?

I tell the Fry,
"Close your eyes, and then
take a deep breath.
Count to ten."

We do the count,

then reach the school.

We are all sleek

and pretty cool.

Off the shark bus,
fin to fin,
we follow Principal Pike
right in.

One guitarist,
one small rapper,
one sole singer,
one shell clapper,
one bell ringer.

Our lobster drummer
looks real pale.
The singer seems slower
than a snail.
I worry if
we're good enough,
or if the band
is going to fail.

That's when our teacher,
with raised reeds,
shows us how
a conductor leads.

We have no time
to worry now.
We play as well
as we know how.

Our practice is done.

We take a break.

But I still worry
there will be a mistake.

The seaweed curtains
start to part.
I feel the tempo
of my heart.

What if a current grabs my strings? What if our soloist never sings?

It's far too late
to leave the stage.
I tremble and try
to read the page.

I close my eyes.
I count to ten.
I strum my sea guitar,
and then . . .

I pluck the strings.

Sole sister sings.

Lobster drums.

My heart . . . well . . . hums.

Principal Pike
begins to clap
his fins together.
Tap. TAP TAP!

And everyone
joins in applause
with fins and shells
and lobster claws.

At last our leader's
reeds all drop—
the signal for the Fry
to stop.

We look around.

We grin with pride.

Fears float away

upon the tide.

We take a bow

for the whole school.

We're BIG fish now,
and we're *real* cool.